LoVe MonSteR

Rachel Bright

WELCOME TO
CUTESVILLE
Home of the fluffy

Farrar Straus Giroux
New York

This
is a mOnster.

(Hello, Monster.)

I think you'll agree,
he's a little bit funny-looking.

To say the least.

He lives in a world of cute, fluffy things,

OFFICIAL PILE
OF
EXTREME
CUTENESS

which makes being
funny-looking...

pretty,

darn

hard.

You might have noticed that **everybody loves**

kittens...

and puppies...

and bunnies.

You know,
cute, fluffy
things.

But nobody loves
a slightly hairy,
I-suppose-a-bit-googly-eyed
monster.

(POor MOnster.)

This might be enough to make a monster
feel, well, a bit down in the dumps.
But not being the moping-around sort,

BIG, WIDE WORLD

he decided to
set out and look
for someone who'd
love him,
just the way he was.

He looked high.

He looked low.

tumbleweed

He looked middle-ish.

He looked inside.

And outside.

More than once he thought that maybe . . .

just maybe . . .

he'd found what he was looking for.

But, as it turned out, things were
never quite as they seemed.

Yes, it would be fair to say that his search did **not** go well.

And then it didn't
go well some more.

It didn't go well for such a long time, in fact,

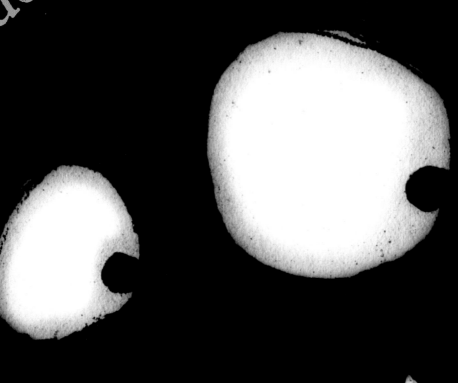

that it began to get

dark.

And
scary.

And, well,

not very nice.

So the **monster**,
having lost **all** his Oomph,
decided it was time to give up,

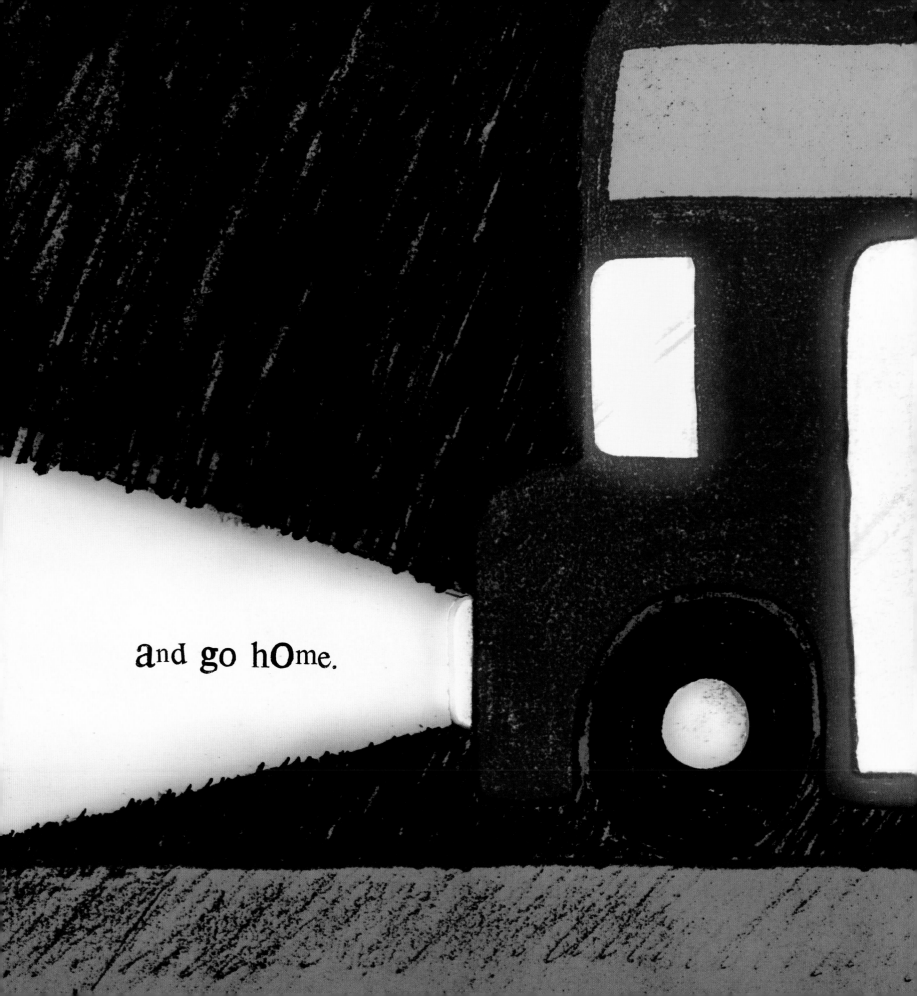

and go hOme.

But in the blink of a gOogly eye . . .

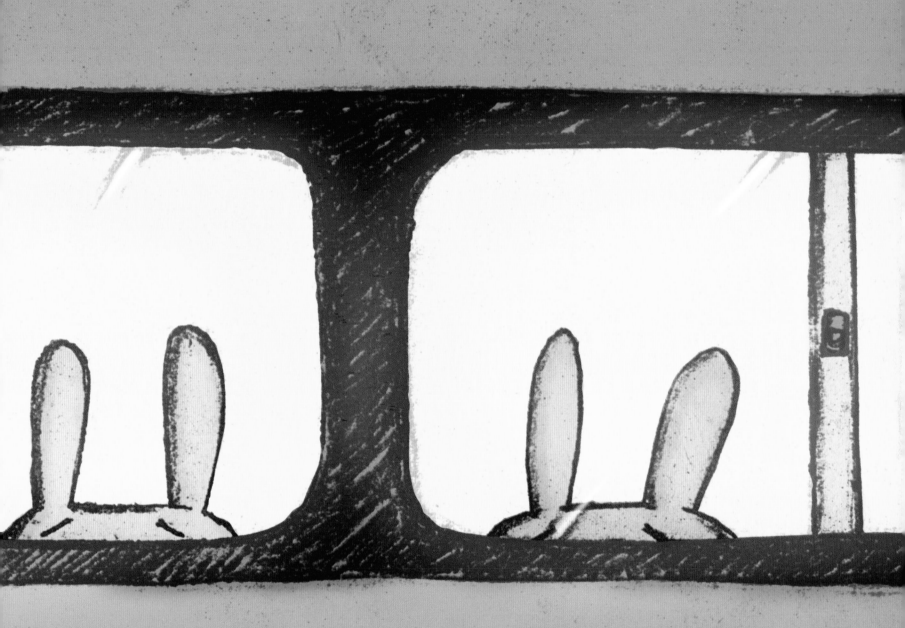

everything
Changed.

You see,
Sometimes,
when you least expect it...

love
finds you.

For the monsters who've found me
(& one slightly hairy one in particular)
–R.B.

And with special
wow-you're-amazing thank-yous to Mandy,
Nancy, Helen, Ann-Janine, Kayt, James & Rose

Farrar Straus Giroux Books for Young Readers
175 Fifth Avenue, New York, 10010

Copyright © 2012 by Rachel Bright
All rights reserved
Printed in China by South China Printing Co. Ltd., Dongguan City, Guangdong Province
First published in Great Britain by HarperCollins Publishers Ltd.
First American edition, 2014
3 5 7 9 10 8 6 4 2

mackids.com

Library of Congress Control Number: 2013941593

ISBN 978-0-374-34646-1

Farrar Straus Giroux Books for Young Readers may be purchased for business or promotional use.
For information on bulk purchases please contact Macmillan Corporate and Premium Sales
Department at (800) 221-7945 x5442 or by email at specialmarkets@macmillan.com.